Deadline

by

John Townsend

Illustrated by Pulsar Studios

You do not need to read this page – just get on with the book!

First published in 2007 in Great Britain by
Barrington Stoke Ltd
18 Walker St, Edinburgh, EH3 7LP

www.barringtonstoke.co.uk

Reprinted 2008

ISBN: 978-1-84299-461-0

Printed in Great Britain by Bell & Bain Ltd

AUTHOR ID

Name: John Townsend

Likes: Edinburgh in August, making marmalade in January, Bach in the bath, anytime

Dislikes: Sprouts, shopping, Christmas (Bah humbug!)

3 words that best describe me: "Bond, James Bond." (In my dreams!)

A secret that not many people know: My appendix was removed when I was six ... and I want it back!

ILLUSTRATOR ID

Name: Jorge from Pulsar Studios

Likes: Comics, manga, music, horror, dogs, trips, martial art movies

Dislikes: Not having enough time to do the things I like!

3 words that best describe me: Lazy, grumpy (not so much), tall

A secret that not many people know: I would like to make a film

To the children of the Tree-House Story Club at Franche School, Kidderminster.

Contents

Barney will be back!
Watch out for his
explosive new adventure

FIREBOMB

Coming soon ... in 2008

Chapter 1
Hiding

The door was open a bit but Barney couldn't see what was inside the room.

He heard someone creeping down the corridor behind him. He had to act fast. He touched the handle. The door swung open and he slid into the room. It was still and dark inside. The window blinds let in just a little light. He could see a big table with blue plastic chairs around it. A flip-chart stood at one end of the room. Barney guessed this was some sort of room for meetings.

A shadow passed across the doorway. Barney dived under the table. He tried not to rattle any chair legs as he scuttled like a lizard over the carpet. He crawled over stale crisps into the dark space under the table. He'd be safe here, with luck. Safe from Laura.

He knew Laura would be looking for him already. "I bet you £5 you can't find me in five minutes," Barney had said, and they'd both set their watches.

Now Barney was safe, hidden under the table. He pressed the button to light up his watch. One minute, 48 seconds had already gone. Laura would never find him here.

He was sure he'd win the bet. But he knew if Mrs Peters found them playing hide-and-seek in the hotel, there'd be big trouble. After what she'd said to him downstairs an hour ago, he knew she'd be really mad!

"Barney Jones, I'd like a word," she'd said. "I know you're the youngest member of this school ski trip but you're 13 and should know better. Silly games in a big hotel are not on. I saw you mucking about in the lift just now. I didn't want to bring you on this trip in the first place, but your parents begged me. You mustn't let them or me down. Do you understand?"

She waited for Barney to look sorry. He did the look so well and most teachers were taken in. He could make himself look like a sweet little puppy. But the look didn't work on Mrs Peters.

She went on, "As you did so well on the dry ski slope, I felt sure you'd fit in with this trip. With your gym skills, I expect great things from you. But if I have to talk to you again, Barney, I shall be very cross."

"Sorry, miss." Barney's sad puppy look still wasn't working. And then Mrs Peters said something which seemed harsh, even for her.

"It's not too late to call your parents. I can tell them to come and take you home, you know."

Why didn't Mrs Peters like him? Barney couldn't work it out. Most adults thought he was a "bright young man with sparkle". They all liked him at Gym Club – but his gym skills and charm just didn't impress her.

She'd been grumpy ever since the ski trip had started to go wrong. They'd had to wait all morning at the airport for the freezing fog to lift. That had got her really stressed. Then the airport announced that all flights to Austria were delayed for another 24 hours. Mrs Peters spent the afternoon trying to book the school party into a hotel down the road from the airport. All the kids sat there, bored, fed up, plugged into iPods, but Mrs Peters was on the phone to the insurance company and the stress showed in her eyes.

The trip had got off to a bad start. As soon as everyone was on the coach at school, Barney's watch alarm went off at full blast. Everyone had laughed. The alarm on his watch made the sound of a crowing cockerel. Mrs Peters hadn't laughed. "If I hear that thing again, Barney Jones, I'll take it off you."

Then things got even worse. Barney's
mum rang him on his mobile that very
minute. Its ring-tone was just as loud and
weird. Barney had downloaded a file called
'gunfight' with shots and a final burst of
machine-gun fire. It was *loud*.

"Switch that thing off right away!" Mrs
Peters barked. They were half way down the

school drive when she told the coach driver to stop so she could shout into the microphone. "Loud childish noises do not belong on my trips, thank you very much," she said. "Nor silly little boys like Barney Jones." She took Barney's mobile from him to keep in her bag.

Barney's knee cracked as he moved under the table. He hoped Laura hadn't heard. The seconds were ticking by but she could still win the game. Was it her who'd just come in to the room? If she looked under the table, she'd see him. Barney waited for her trainers to appear beside him ... but instead he saw someone else's legs.

A man's black polished shoes and dark trousers with turn-ups.

Barney heard the door close and another pair of feet, this time in sandals, stood at the end of the table by the flip-chart. Barney held his breath as the black shoes squeaked right by his hand. His fingers were so tense now that they didn't even feel a cold gooey slice of mushroom that lay squashed into the carpet. This was no place to hide. It wasn't a place where he wanted to be found. Not now.

Chapter 2
Ticking Seconds

Barney curled up into a ball to try and make himself vanish.

"Right, we haven't got long," the man in the black shoes said. He spoke as if he was in a hurry and didn't want anyone to hear what he was saying. "Here's the key to 829."

There was a loud noise above Barney's head as keys clattered on the table.

"You'll find all you need – telescope, radios, timetables. Keep checking the internet, too. This fog has messed things up but now we've got some extra time. They'll give out the plane's new take-off time soon. You'll see the end of the runway from the window once the fog clears."

The keys scraped across the table. The sandals moved closer. Barney smelled sweaty feet as another man began to speak. Barney could tell the man didn't speak English very well. "And the motorbike? I need to get away fast," he said.

"It's in the basement. Everything's ready. No probs."

Suddenly the keys fell to the floor and bounced onto Barney's hand. It startled him so much he almost yelped. There were two keys on a key ring, with the number tag – 829. Barney didn't stop to think. He flicked his hand and the keys flipped across the carpet and jangled against the black shoes.

Barney held his breath again. Keys don't normally fall to the floor and bounce like that. Would the men guess there was someone hidden under the table? How would he explain what he was doing down there?

A hand came down to pick up the keys. The face of the man in the black shoes was almost level with the table-top as he grunted and groped to touch the keys. Barney couldn't stop looking at the man's hand. It was a right hand ... with the thumb missing.

A voice boomed into Barney's ear and filled the space around him.

"Make sure you keep that gun loaded at all times. Never open the door to anyone. Only me. I'll tap the code. And don't leave any finger prints. MI5 will look all over this hotel and they'll have DNA on file."

The voice went soft again as at last the man stood up again. He'd picked up the keys without even looking under the table. Barney couldn't breathe. He could still see that hand with no thumb in his mind.

"This room is where we'll meet to make progress checks. If you get six sharp knocks on your door and then a gap, and then another knock, it means get down here fast. Right? Any questions?"

"Er ... I think no. I kill first – ask question later."

Barney just wanted the men to go now. He knew he'd already heard too much and was in the middle of something scary. His puppy eyes look wouldn't work on these men. He'd only heard a few minutes of their talk and it didn't make sense. But he knew he'd be in big trouble if they found him.

In fact, Barney had been under the table for too long. It wasn't safe. His watch was still ticking towards its five-minute deadline. That was when his alarm would go off to show the end of the game he was playing with Laura. There were just 16 seconds left before his watch would blast the sound of a crowing cockerel. But Barney had forgotten about that, as the black shoes headed for the door and turned.

"Another thing. Always keep the *Do Not Disturb* sign on your door."

15 seconds left.

"You not worry. No one will get in that room," the sandal-man said.

13 seconds.

"What was that?"

"What?"

"A noise. Someone's there."

"Where?"

"Just outside."

The sandal-man pulled the door open. Barney heard a woman's voice.

"There's a phone call for you down at the desk, sir," the woman said.

"Right. I'll be down," the man with no thumb said. He sounded calm.

Eight seconds left.

"You think she heard anything?" Sandal-man was up-tight.

"Relax. If I find she knows anything, I'll deal with her."

Four seconds left.

Both sets of feet walked out of the room and the door clicked shut behind them – just as Barney's watch blurted its cockerel alarm. Barney slammed his hand down on the alarm button so fast he banged his head on the table and then there was silence. Apart from his thumping heart.

The door flew open. "You hear that?" Sandal-man marched into the room.

"Relax. You're too jumpy for your own good. It was something outside the window. The place is full of kids."

"Hmm." Sandal-man didn't sound so sure. He stood for some seconds before he turned, backed out through the door and slammed it behind him.

The room was empty again. Barney lay face-down with a sigh. The half-eaten sausage by his cheek didn't bother him. He didn't move for a full two minutes. His head was in a whirl. He was still lying in a daze when Laura found him.

Chapter 3
Time To Act

"You've got a simple choice," Laura told Barney. "Either you tell Mrs Peters you've overheard some dodgy men who might be up to something odd. Or you report them to the hotel. There's a security man in the lobby. Or you shut up and pretend nothing happened. That's pretty simple, isn't it?"

Barney thought. "I've already made up my mind. If I tell Mrs Peters, she'll just send me home." He spoke in her voice – "'You've been messing about and your childish stories are getting the better of you. We're all tired. You're just a silly little boy. I'll have to phone your parents, Barney Jones.'" He was a perfect mimic.

Laura smiled. But Barney wasn't joking. Her other idea was no good either.

"It's no good telling Security," he said to her. "That's a waste of time. I'd just be seen as 'Kid with daft ideas. Hears strange men. No proof.' Anyway, they'd be sure to tell Mrs Peters. Look, Laura, I can't prove anything but I tell you – there's something weird going on."

Laura looked at his eyes. They weren't soft and like a puppy's now. They were hard-set. "I can tell you're not going to forget all about this," she said.

"I can't, Laura. It was the sound in Sandal-man's voice. He's evil. He's plotting something terrible. I know it. I've got to do something. I must find out what he's up to and then I can tell Security. If I had a bit of proof, I'd be able to give a few facts. I need to look in Room 829 for myself."

Laura didn't look so sure. "But if what you say is true, there could be a man in Room 829. A man with a gun who seems happy to use it."

"I know," Barney said. "I've already got a plan. And the thing is, I need you to help me."

"OK. As long as I can borrow your cool watch when we go skiing. I love that cockerel alarm. It's so loud. I might just leave it in Mrs Peters' bedroom and set it for two in the morning!"

Barney smiled at the idea but at that moment he had something else to worry about. He needed to think hard. How could he tell Security about Sandal-man in a way which would make them listen to him? And who was the man with no thumb? Sandal-man and No-Thumb. It sounded like the title of a weird film.

"Can I borrow your mobile?" he asked Laura. "I need it to take some pictures. When I get a bit of proof of whatever's going on, I can hand it over to Security and they'll believe me."

"Is that all you need me for, just my mobile?" Laura grumbled.

"I think we could use your acting talent, Laura," Barney went on. "Can you pretend to be a cleaner? This hotel is full of students working as cleaners. I found a cleaning cupboard on our landing when I was looking for somewhere to hide. We can get you an outfit and all the kit. Then maybe you can get something for me."

"Sounds fine to me. What do you want?" Laura asked.

"Just a key. The key to Room 829."

****

Half an hour later, Barney sat in the entrance hall of the hotel. There was a lot going on. Taxis were coming and going; people were rushing about or just standing around waiting. Because of all the flight delays, the hotel was packed. A voice crackled over the loud-speakers. A few flights to the US were going to take off soon but most of the other flights had been delayed for 24 hours.

Barney watched the swirling crowds. He had found a seat by a drinks machine. A man at the security desk was trying to help a woman who had lost something but she spoke no English. Someone else sat reading a newspaper. Barney looked over and saw the headline – "*Fears of Airport Attack.*" For the first time Barney started to think ... what if? What had he heard upstairs? Or was he just getting carried away? Maybe the two men up in the room where he'd hidden were fooling about. Maybe he was making a fuss over nothing ... Barney snapped back to the here and now. Someone was asking him something.

"I hope you is enjoying your stay, sir. But please, no play in the lifts." Barney looked up at the room-maid and moved his feet to let her sweep the floor. Then he worked out who she was. He stopped himself from giggling. It was Laura! She looked great in her overall, head scarf and with a bucket full of dusters!

"Follow me, sir." Laura walked into one of the lifts and Barney followed a few steps behind. He was still trying not to laugh. Only when the doors closed and they were alone in the lift did they talk.

"Here it is," she said with a proud grin. She held up a door key with the tag – 829.

"I had to sign for it and I thought they'd work out I was a fake. But everyone's so busy, no one took any notice of me. I just told someone I'd shut my key in the room and needed to borrow a spare key for two minutes. It was dead simple. Here you are, Barney. Now it's over to you. I had the easy bit."

She handed Barney the key as the lift stopped at the top floor and the doors slid open. Room 829 was somewhere down the long dark corridor ahead ... a tunnel of blue carpet and closed doors. A tunnel into the unknown.

Chapter 4
Room 829

The corridor was silent. At the far end Barney found the door marked 829. It had a sign hanging from the handle – **DO NOT DISTURB.** But that was just what he was going to do. His hands were sweating and his throat felt tight.

The plan was simple. Barney would knock six times on the door, then he'd wait

for a moment and knock again after a gap.
Then he'd run into the cleaning cupboard
down the corridor. Laura was already
hiding there. It took one and a half minutes
to get down to the conference room two
floors below. Laura and Barney had already
timed it. Sandal-man would walk past the
cupboard and be gone for three minutes.
That was all the time Barney had to get
inside Room 829, take pictures with Laura's
mobile and sneak out to hide in the
cupboard again. He had to do all that
before Sandal-man came back. Laura would
keep watch and if Sandal-man was back
early, she'd switch on the Hoover. The noise
would warn Barney to come out fast, and
run for it.

Barney took a deep breath and lifted his
fist. Knock, knock, knock, knock, knock,
knock ... wait ... knock. Run! He dashed to
the cupboard, threw himself inside, and
Laura pulled the door shut, leaving a tiny

crack to peep through. Sandal-man was already outside, looking around. He stomped past the cupboard, headed down the corridor and vanished into the lift. With Laura's mobile in one hand and the key in the other, Barney ran back to Room 829.

Once inside the room, Barney began to look over all the clutter on the bed. There were maps and plans everywhere. Barney thought they looked like maps of airport runways. Notepads had scribbled workings-out of angles and distances. A laptop showed a list of flight times and details. It said: **Flight RS 621 to Washington delayed. New departure time to be announced.**

Barney clicked the mobile's camera button, turned and knocked a plate of chips on the floor. He tried to clear them up, and got his fingers covered in ketchup. Time was running out and he'd still found nothing that would really show the police that anything was wrong.

It was then Barney saw the barrel of a big gun under the bed. He stepped back in shock and slipped on the papers that were all over the floor. A leaflet showed a weapon called 'Igla – 9K38'. 'PAMS', he read. 'Portable Anti-Aircraft Missile System.' He pressed the mobile button with his sticky finger. The camera flash lit up the room as he caught sight of himself in a mirror. There was ketchup on his top lip. He looked as if he'd had a nose-bleed.

There was little time left and it was just too risky to pull the weapon from under the bed for him to take a clear picture. Then Barney saw newspaper cuttings in different languages scattered on a chair. A scribbled note lay on top. Barney had no idea what the note said but he lifted the mobile again.

Flash. He looked at his watch. Less than 30 seconds left.

Laura was still standing outside the room. She looked up from her watch and gave a gasp. She was looking right into a man's angry eyes.

"What you do here?" he shouted. "Can't you read? It say do not disturb."

Laura's foot pushed the button of the Hoover but Sandal-man ripped its plug from the socket.

"I said 'no disturb'. Go. Get out of here." He pushed his key in the door and kicked it open.

"So sorry, mister," Laura muttered. She dropped the flex at his feet. It caught his sandal and he turned angrily.

"You stupid fool. Get out of here." He lifted his fist as if he was going to hit her.

Laura was desperate to give Barney a few more seconds to get out. "Sorry, I no understand," she said. "What you say, mister?"

Sandal-man kicked the Hoover across the corridor, turned and pushed into the room. He slammed the door behind him and the **DO NOT DISTURB** sign fell down to the floor. Laura's heart was pounding. She'd failed. Barney hadn't got out in time. He was still trapped inside.

As soon as Barney heard the key in the door, he froze. What could he do? There was nowhere to hide. With no time to think, he ran to the window. There was a little balcony outside. By the time Sandal-man burst in, Barney was out there, stuffing the mobile in his pocket.

He looked down to the car park far below. The cars looked like tiny toys from where he was. This was the top floor – eight floors up. There was no escape – but he had to get away before Sandal-man saw him.

Without stopping to plan his next move, Barney gripped the rails of the balcony and flipped himself over, dangling his legs from the ledge. He clung on tight and tried to see the balcony below. Luckily, it stuck out a bit. That would make it easier for him to drop onto.

His fingers began to slip with the greasy ketchup on his hands. He tried to swing his legs so he wouldn't hit the railings as he dropped. His life depended on his gym skills. But then he'd always been good on the parallel bars and the box. But this was far more scary.

A noise in the room above made him let go.

Barney swung and dropped. A chunk of brick flew out into mid air. He landed on the balcony below with a thud. He stood up and tried to open the windows. He couldn't believe his luck when the window slid open and he stepped inside the room. He heard a woman singing in the shower as he crept across the carpet. Just as he got to the door to the corridor, the bathroom door opened and a woman stepped out, wrapped in a towel. She screamed.

Barney muttered, "Very sorry, madam!" and ran from the room. Even after he'd darted down the corridor, he could still hear the woman's shouts.

"Help, there's a Peeping Tom out here! He's got a camera too!" she was yelling.

If he hadn't been in such a hurry, Barney would have laughed about being called a Peeping Tom. But he just had to find Laura and tell her what he'd found in Room 829. He'd been right to be scared. Sandal-man was a terrorist ... and Barney was sure he was about to strike.

Chapter 5
Race Against Time

Laura looked at each photo on her mobile. The one that puzzled them most was the note in French.

Date limite
Ven?
Vol RS 621
Tire de toit de 829

"What does all that mean?" she asked.

"I don't know but I'm sure they're going to shoot down a plane. Why else would they have all those flight details and that stuff on surface-to-air missiles? It can mean only one thing. Sandal-man plans to bring down that flight to Washington. That's what the RS 621 stands for on the notepad. I saw it on his laptop. That's the flight number of the plane that's going to Washington."

"You'll have to tell Mrs Peters now," Laura said.

Barney thought. "I'd rather you did. She'll listen to you more than me. Can you use your mobile to check the internet about that Igla missile thing? Then I'll show the photos on your mobile to Hotel Security. I'll tell them they've got to stop Sandal-man before it's too late. I'll meet you back here in 15 minutes."

The man at the Security Desk wore a crisp white shirt, black tie and navy jumper. Barney asked him if they could talk in private.

"Sure, son. Come through into my office." The man led him to a room with a wall of TV screens. He could see what all the CCTV cameras around the hotel were filming. "Take a seat, lad," the man went on.

"I've found a plot to shoot down a flight to Washington," Barney began. "I think the plane's due to take off as soon as the fog clears. A man in Room 829 has got a missile and a gun. He's really scary and he'll kill anyone who gets in his way. He's got maps of flight-paths and stuff. You've got to believe me. Someone's got to do something."

The man leaned against a desk, folded his arms and thought for a while.

"I see. Keep calm, you've done the right thing. I believe you, young man," he said.

"Great. What a relief," Barney said with a sigh. "I thought you'd think I'm a nutter."

"Not at all. What you say makes perfect sense to me. I'll just have to write down a few details. Do your parents know you've come to see me?"

"No. No one knows," said Barney. "That is, apart from my friend Laura. She's got the photos of Room 829 on her mobile. I'm not with my parents. Mrs Peters is in charge of our school trip but I haven't told her yet."

"Write down your name and room number for me," the security man said. "Then I'll get our guys to check this out."

"Make sure they know Sandal-man is dangerous. He's not alone, either. There's a guy with shiny black shoes with him."

The man leaned forward to offer Barney his pen. It was then that Barney froze. The man's thumb was missing.

"Something the matter, son?"

Barney couldn't speak. He looked down at the man's shiny black shoes and turn-ups. Just then he saw one of the screens flicker in front of him. It was exactly the same as on Sandal-man's laptop. *Flight RS 621 to Washington delayed. Now departing 22.43.*

Barney saw the blow coming out of the corner of his eye. The man's fist came right at him as Barney ducked, grabbed a glass paper-weight from the desk and threw it at the man's head. It cracked into his ear. The man groaned and crumpled to the floor. Barney didn't wait to see what happened next. He ran through the door and darted up the stairs. He looked at his watch. It was past ten o'clock. Although he didn't have a clue what to do now, he knew one thing for sure. Whatever was about to happen, he had less than half an hour before the plane to Washington took off. He had to save it!

Chapter 6
No Time To Lose

"OK, stay cool," Laura told Barney. "Let's just think about this. We've got to act fast but we're on our own. Mrs Peters is no good. She told me I was crazy and that you were in deep trouble."

"What have I done now?"

"The woman you saw in her bathroom reported you to the hotel. She described your shirt exactly and Mrs Peters is after you. Big time."

"I don't care about her. That flight to Washington takes off at 22.43. It just came up on the screen. That's in 15 minutes. But that's all we know. What can we do, Laura?"

Laura held up her mobile. "I've done something that helps. I showed Anabelle from school the photo of that note in French. Her mum's French so she helped me work what it means out."

Date limite
Ven?
Vol RS 621
Tire de toit de 829

"She says *Ven* must mean *vendredi*. That's Friday – tonight. *Vol* is the flight number."

"Yeah, big deal!" Barney shouted. "We know all that already! What we need to know is where will Sandal-man fire his missile from. If we don't know that, we can't stop him."

"Anabelle told me '*Tire de 829*' means 'Shoot from 829.' Room 829. The '*toit*' bit must be short for 'toilet'. I guess he's going to fire the missile from the toilet window."

"Don't be daft. He can't fire a huge missile from there."

Laura looked scared. "He can, you know. I've just searched the Internet. Look."

She showed the details on her mobile:

The missile is fired by a gunner from the shoulder in a standing or kneeling position. PAMS Igla has a homing head. It can find its target and will hit in seconds.

Barney looked at his watch. "If we don't do something fast, that missile is going to kill hundreds of passengers. I'm setting my alarm now. We've got 12 minutes to the deadline."

Barney took the key to Room 829 out of his pocket. "I'm going back in there. Call the police. And call the airport. Tell them to stop the plane from taking off."

"It's no use calling the airport, I've already tried. All I get is an answer-machine that puts you 'on hold'. Everyone's phoning the airport. No one answers. Barney, you can't go in Room 829. Not with Sandal-man in there. Not on your own."

"I'll be careful. Why don't you come to back me up? You can bring your mobile. We need a mobile and Mrs Peters has taken mine."

Laura smiled. "Hey! Give me some credit." She handed Barney his own mobile. "I thought you might need this. Mrs Peters left it on the table beside her ... it was simple!"

"Laura, that's really cool. Well done. Now we've got to get up to Room 829. Quick!"

They ran to the lift. There was just ten minutes to the deadline. "I'll try their secret knock again," Barney said. "If we can get Sandal-man to come out of Room 829, I can grab his missile-launcher."

Laura hid in the cupboard again and Barney knocked on the door. Then he ran to join her. She peeped out but no one came out of the room. Nothing.

Six minutes left.

Barney held the key to Room 829. "I'll just have to go in and hope for the best. Keep watch outside and warn me if anyone comes."

Laura looked at her mobile. There were less than six minutes left. "I'll phone you if you're not out by the deadline," she said. "Take care, Barney ... *please.*"

Chapter 7
Count Down

Barney pushed the key into the door very slowly. He opened the door softly and peered inside. Room 829 was empty. It looked as if no one had ever been here. Barney listened outside the toilet. Nothing. He eased the door open a crack. There was no one there. There wasn't even a window. Barney's heart sank. Sandal-man must be going to fire the missile from somewhere else after all. He was too late.

Five minutes left.

As Barney turned to leave the room, he felt a breeze on his face. The curtains at the French window moved. He went over to look out at the balcony. Nothing.

He stepped out to peer over the edge. The fog had almost gone and he could look across to the airport and see the runway lights. It was then he saw something move just above him. There was a rope hanging from the roof above the balcony.

Four minutes.

Barney gripped the rope and began to climb. The ropes and wall bars at the gym were nothing like as scary as this. He dangled in the air eight floors up in a freezing wind. His fingers were numb.

When he got to the top, Barney tried to lift himself onto the edge of the roof. He peered across the wide flat roof to the far side. There was a figure kneeling there … with the missile-launcher.

Three minutes.

Sandal-man was aiming a missile at the distant runway. His back was turned as Barney scrambled to get his knee up over the gutter. Suddenly a chunk of gutter snapped off with a crack and Barney slipped. His hands grabbed at the rope as his feet swung out over the spinning car park. His fingernails dug into the rope, and his heart thumped in his chest. Once again he tried to pull himself up to the roof and clamber over the gutter.

Two minutes.

Barney pulled himself up and rolled onto the roof.

The cold wind cut into him. He didn't dare stand up near the edge of the roof – a gust could sweep him right off and fling him down to the car park far below. He crawled across the roof, towards Sandal-man. He didn't know what he was going to do but somehow he just had to stop that missile going off.

One minute.

Already Barney could hear a plane beginning to taxi along the runway. Sandal-man shifted the missile-launcher and pointed it at the sky above the red lights at the end of the runway. Barney looked at his watch as the last few seconds slipped away.

He pulled the watch off his wrist and hurled it at Sandal-man. It clattered at his feet and startled him. He looked round. His wild eyes stared back at Barney. He yelled and then turned back, ready to fire at the plane that was speeding down the runway.

Suddenly the watch at the man's feet screeched its alarm. Sandal-man stumbled in surprise – and Barney threw himself at him.

The missile-launcher clattered down to their feet. It gave a roar and clouds of smoke engulfed the two of them. A rocket screamed out across the roof in a jet of sparks. Like a firework, it shot out into the sky before diving down in an angry spiral ... zooming down to the car park. It shot into the roof of a van and exploded with a shower of flames and a plume of black smoke.

The bang was drowned by another roar – a jumbo jet rose up into the sky and soared right over them. It vanished into the clouds.

Sandal-man yelled with rage. He pulled out a gun and kicked Barney across the roof. Barney fell with a thud, rolled over and scuttled towards the edge. Sandal-man lifted the gun and took aim. A bullet smashed into the roof by Barney's head. The next wouldn't miss.

Barney saw the rope he'd climbed up. He made a dive for it. His mobile and coins scattered from his pockets. He hurled himself at the rope, twisting and grabbing madly in the air. He held on to the rope as he swung back and smashed into the wall. The rope began to split ... Sandal-man stood above him, with the gun aimed at his head.

Barney looked up into Sandal-man's cold eyes as the rope gave way. He fell to the balcony below. He lay, stunned and an easy target. Sandal-man touched the trigger.

Suddenly a rally of gun-shots ripped out across the roof. Sandal-man spun round, stumbling. Everything happened so quickly. Sandal-man screamed as he slipped off the edge, falling and cracking his head on the balcony railings before dropping silently to the ground far below. He thudded on the tarmac and lay still, just in front of two police cars that screamed to a halt in the car park.

Barney looked down. He felt sick and blood was dripping from his nose. There was a hand on his shoulder. He turned to see who it was. Laura.

"Am I glad to see you!" she said. "I just called you on your mobile and there was no answer."

"I'm glad you did that," Barney said. "You set off my gun-shots ring. Your timing was perfect. Sandal-man was about to kill me."

"I called you because I had a text from Anabelle. *'Toit'* doesn't mean toilet at all. It's French for – "

"Roof?"

"How did you know? I've called the police too." Laura led Barney back into the bedroom. A man lay grunting and wriggling on the floor. He was tied up tightly with a long flex, and the Hoover was on top of him.

Laura smiled. "That Security guy tried to grab me but I had other ideas for Mr No-Thumb. He was still a bit woozy from your paper-weight. So I just gave him a thump on the other side of his head. I took the Hoover out of the cupboard and smashed him on the ear with the plug!"

Suddenly Mrs Peters burst into the room. She was mad with anger ... and beside her stood two policemen with guns.

Chapter 8
Running Late

Barney and Laura had to write endless statements for the police. There were hours of interviews. The newspapers, television and radio all wanted to know what had happened.

The next morning Barney's parents and Laura's dad arrived at the airport hotel. Just in time for Mrs Peters to take her school ski trip off to Austria. A few days later the police lent Barney and Laura a plane so they could join the school trip for the second half of the week. As they landed in Austria, they joked about what Mrs Peters would say to them.

"Let's hope she doesn't come to meet us in one of her bad moods," Barney said. "I bet she'll tell us off for all the stress we gave her."

But it wasn't like that at all. Mrs Peters greeted them with a big smile. She even giggled in the taxi on the way to their hotel.

"It seems I might have been wrong about you, Barney," she said. "It looks like you've been a very brave boy and you've saved hundreds of lives. I'm very proud of you."

Barney almost choked. It was the first time she'd spoken to him without nagging.

She showed him the headlines in the papers.

Crowing Cockerel Watch Comes Home to Roost.

Lucky Gym Boy Saves Jumbo.

Superboy Hangs by a Thread.

Lifeline Snaps After Deadline.

Mrs Peters held out her hand.

"Even so," she said, "you can give me back your mobile for safe-keeping. Just in case. After all, I wouldn't want you to get into any more trouble because of silly noises."

Before he could stop himself, Barney blew the loudest of farting noises. The taxi driver turned and stared at Barney and the car hit the kerb.

Barney laughed. "Just wait till I get that noise for my next alarm!"

"Not on my ski trip you won't," Mrs Peters snapped.

"Boys will always be boys," Laura giggled. "Just as well if you ask me!"

The taxi pulled up outside the hotel as Barney looked up at the snow-topped mountains beyond. He felt pleased with himself. This was great. He just couldn't wait to run into the hotel. After all, they still had a game of hide-and-seek to finish.

Barrington Stoke would like to thank all its readers for commenting on the manuscript before publication and in particular:

Jodie Lee Bedford
Zoe Burns
Louise Carberry
Susan Irwin
Ann Marie Masterson
Ayisha O'Neill
Eileen Quinn
Roisin Ramsey
Amanda Turner

Become a Consultant!

Would you like to give us feedback on our titles before they are published? Contact us at the email address below – we'd love to hear from you!

info@barringtonstoke.co.uk
www.barringtonstoke.co.uk